DICK KING-SMITH

The Trouble with Edward

illustrated by
Jacqui Thomas

KNIGHT BOOKS
Hodder and Stoughton

Text copyright © Foxbusters Ltd. 1989
Illustrations copyright © Hodder & Stoughton
Ltd. 1989

First published 1989 by Hodder & Stoughton
Children's Books
Knight Books Edition 1991

Printed and bound in Great Britain for
Hodder and Stoughton Children's Books, a
division of Hodder and Stoughton Ltd., Mill
Road, Dunton Green, Sevenoaks, Kent TN13
2YA. (Editorial Office: 47 Bedford Square,
London WC1B 3DP) by T. J. Press (Padstow)
Ltd., Padstow, Cornwall.

British Library C.I.P.

King-Smith, Dick
  The trouble with Edward.
  I. Title   II. Thomas, Jacqui   III. Series
823'.914 [J]

  ISBN 0 340 54616 6

1 **The New Baby**

'You can't call him Edward,' said Mr Bear.

'You can't *not* call him Edward,' said
Mrs Bear, cuddling her newborn baby.
'With a surname like ours everyone will
call him Teddy anyway, so we might just
as well.'

So they called their son Edward Bear.

And sure enough, next day, when
Mr Bear went to the office where he
worked, they said, 'Has your missus had
the baby?'

'Yes.'

'Boy or girl?'

'Boy.'

'What're you going to call him?'

'Edward.'

'Teddy Bear!' everyone shouted. 'Isn't
that lovely!'

'Aren't you lovely!' said Mrs Bear,

stroking the baby's head. 'You've got a lot of hair already, and not only on your head either,' for little Edward Bear's body was covered — if you looked very closely — with a fine down of red-gold hairs.

'And you've got a big strong nose,' said Mrs Bear proudly, 'and the quaintest ears,' and indeed little Edward's ears were smaller and rounder and higher up on the sides of his head than is usual.

That evening Mr and Mrs Bear had
quite a laugh. On his way home from work
Mr Bear had gone into a toyshop and
bought a bright blue teddy bear: it was
quite a big one, the same size, in fact,
as the newborn baby.

Now the parents stood together gazing
down into the cot, smiling at the sight of
the two figures that lay in it. Face to face,
nose to nose indeed, were the two Teddy
Bears, the boy and the toy.

'Good job I got a blue one!' laughed
Mr Bear. 'Otherwise we might have had a
job telling them apart!'

'Oh, what an awful thing to say!' giggled
Mrs Bear, and she gently stroked her
baby's ginger head. Little Edward growled
softly in his sleep.

Edward Bear had been quite a normal weight at birth, but he began to grow very quickly, to grow heavier and to grow stronger.

When he was no more than a few weeks old, his grandfather bent over the cot and put out his finger (as people do, to feel the gentle grasp of a baby's fat little hand), and then gave a gasp, while his pipe fell out of his mouth. The baby let go, and the grandfather stared in amazement at a finger turned quite white and squashed-looking.

'Young Edward,' he said to Mrs Bear later, 'is as strong as a lion, you know!'

'As strong as a bear, you mean!' she said proudly.

But before long pride began to give way to worry.

2 **Early Days**

One day Mrs Bear came into the room to find Edward standing bolt upright in his cot, grasping the bars firmly in his hands.

What huge hands they are, she thought, and 'Whatever are you doing standing up at your age, Teddy?' she said. 'No baby of three months should be able to stand.'

Edward Bear stared through the bars at her with his black boot-button eyes.

He said nothing, for he could not talk, but
he growled a little, and a growl, Mrs Bear
knew, meant that he was hungry, so she
hurried to fetch her son a spoonful of
honey.

'I'm worried,' she said to Mr Bear, when he came home from the office. 'Edward was standing up today.'

'He's just very advanced,' said Mr Bear in a pleased sort of voice, looking down at his sleeping son.

'But he's crazy about honey,' said Mrs Bear. 'He eats more honey than anything else. It can't be good for his teeth. And he's got an awful lot of teeth already.'

'All the better to bite you with!' said Mr Bear in a jokey sort of voice.

'It isn't funny,' said Mrs Bear. 'Just look at this,' and she picked Edward's teddy bear out of the cot. Patches of its blue fur were missing, one of its ears was almost bitten off and, as for its body, it looked as though it had been run over by a steam-roller.

'Well, he's just chewed it a bit,' said Mr Bear in a doubtful sort of voice, 'and he hugs it at night, doesn't he, like all babies do.'

'All babies don't have a hug like that,' said Mrs Bear.

But any chance that Mr and Mrs Bear might have had of persuading each other that Edward was just a normal baby disappeared very shortly.

Edward had been born in April and by now he was seven months old. Winter came early that year, and by mid-November the weather was becoming bitterly cold, with icy winds and night frosts and forecasts of snow.

And one morning (when it had actually begun to snow) Mrs Bear went to wake Edward — and couldn't.

'I can't wake Teddy!' she cried to her husband. 'I've shaken him, I've shouted at him, he stays fast asleep!'

Mr Bear phoned the doctor.

'I've never before come across such a case,' said the doctor after he had examined the sleeping baby.

'What's wrong with him?' cried the Bears.

'Nothing,' said the doctor, 'that I can find. His temperature is sub-normal, to be sure, and his heart-rate has slowed considerably,

but otherwise Edward is a perfectly
healthy baby.' He paused, rubbing his chin
in thought. 'Edward,' he said. 'Hm . . .
I suppose you call him Teddy, Mrs Bear?'

'Yes,' said Mrs Bear.

'Strange,' said the doctor.

'But what's the matter with him, doctor?'
said Mr Bear.

'Your son,' said the doctor, 'is in a state
of hibernation.'

3 **Growing Up**

Edward slept solidly for five months.
He woke again as winter gave way to
springtime; just before his first birthday,
he suddenly opened his black boot-button
eyes, yawned, scratched, and then
climbed easily up and over the bars of his

cot. He crossed the room at a lumbering run, not crawling on hands and knees as babies usually do, but running on hands and feet, bottom stuck up in the air. Then he reared upright, opened the door and, curling himself up, rolled like a ball down the stairs and galloped into the kitchen where his parents sat at breakfast.

'Teddy!' gasped Mrs Bear, 'You're awake!'

'Grrr,' said her son.

'Don't speak to your mother like that, you young cub!' said Mr Bear, but Edward only growled more loudly and fiercely, and would not stop until Mrs Bear

hurriedly produced a jar of honey and began to spoon it into his open jaws.

'He's ravenous!' she said, as the honey disappeared. 'He's had nothing to eat for five months, poor lamb!'

23

'I don't know about "lamb"', said
Mr Bear, watching in amazement as
Edward then ate a pot of strawberry jam,
a packet of chocolate biscuits and a tin of
pilchards. Sweet things — and fish — had
always been his favourites, but now he

showed that anything edible was welcome.
Mrs Bear's supermarket bill doubled,
and Edward's growth kept pace with it.

When winter drew near once more and
it was almost time to hibernate again,
no one outside the family would have
recognised this powerful youngster,
his inside layered with fat against the long
sleep, his outside generously covered now
with a ginger fur.

In fact no one outside the family set
eyes on him, for Mrs Bear no longer took
him out in his pram. Two nosey ladies had

peered into it once, and she had heard
them talking to each other afterwards:

'Whatever is the world coming to!'

'A grown woman pushing a pram with a
great teddy bear in it!'

After that she left Edward in the garden
when she went out. Although he still did
not speak, he had an assortment of noises
to show his feelings. Growling expressed
anger as well as hunger, a grunt meant
'All right, I understand', and when he was
pleased he made a kind of sing-song
whining sound.

Luckily the Bear garden had several tall
leafy trees in it, which Edward loved to
climb. And what a climber he was! With
much the same hands-and-feet action by
which he normally progressed on the
level, he would run up the trunks with
amazing speed and sit happily perched in
the highest branches.

'Stay in the garden, Teddy,' Mrs Bear
would say.

Grunt.

'And if you promise to be a good boy,
you can climb the trees,' and, whining with
pleasure, up he would go.

So time went by, and Edward Bear grew larger and stronger and hairier. Each year he retired to his bed at the onset of winter and did not wake until the violets and primroses were blooming and the call of the cuckoo was heard again.

Each year also he seemed less inclined to stay indoors (apart from hibernation time) and would spend every possible hour in the garden. Mostly he lumbered about with his strange four-legged run, or climbed about in the trees, but Mrs Bear had to put up with the fact that

he liked digging things up with his hands
and eating them; not only her potatoes
and carrots suffered in this way but also
all sorts of bulbs which Edward seemed to
find very tasty. Wet weather did not
trouble him for the ever-thickening
covering of ginger hair on his body
seemed to be waterproof.

4 **A Bear-Hug**

When he was four, Mrs Bear said to
Mr Bear, 'He'll soon be old enough to go
to school. What are we to do? He's never
met any other children, and he won't be
able to talk to them. And how are we
going to explain to the school that he'll be
away for half the winter term and all of the
spring?' But in fact they never had to face
the problem.

One day in late August, when Edward
was nearly four and a half years old and
as big as and much stronger than a boy of
twelve, his grandmother was playing with
him on the lawn. They were playing a
game with fir-cones, a game that Edward
seemed to like, lining them up in rows on
the grass. His grandmother used to point
to them and count 'One-two-three-four...',

hoping that this might inspire her grandson to speech, even perhaps to learning his numbers. But often the game did not last long, for Edward would eat the fir-cones.

On this particular day Edward's grandmother forgot the rule that all the Bear family had learned, namely that you could not speak to Edward as you would to an ordinary child. You had to be careful. He was so strong.

But she forgot, and looking at him
standing there dressed only in a pair of
shorts, so beautifully muscular and
powerful with the sunshine glinting on his
ginger fur — bare-headed, bare-chested,
bare-footed, as strong as a . . .

'Oh,' she cried, 'oh, my little Teddy!
Come and give your old granny a big
hug!'

Mr Bear came rushing home from the

office as soon as Mrs Bear telephoned,
but by the time he got there,
the ambulance had taken his mother to
hospital. In fact the doctors never knew
how old Mrs Bear had cracked three ribs
— she told them it was a fall — but
Edward's parents looked at one another
and they knew that the time had come.

It was something that they had
discussed between themselves many
many times, for as year succeeded year
and hibernation followed hibernation and
Teddy Bear, more and more, lived up to

his name, they knew that one day they would have to put into operation the plan that they had made.

Now that day was here.

'Edward!' called his father, and watched as his son came clambering swiftly backwards down the trunk of the tallest tree, and galloped on hands and feet across the lawn towards them, and reared up to his full height, arms outspread.

Mr Bear took a couple of hasty steps back. 'How would you like a treat?' he said.

'We're going on an outing,' said
Mrs Bear. 'To the Safari Park. Come along
now, hold my hand, but gently, mind,'
and off they went to the car.

Now Edward had not been in the car
since a day when his mother had left him
in it at the age of two while she did some
shopping, and had come back to find that
he had pulled the steering-wheel off its
column. So he gave his sing-song whine of
delight at the treat in store, and licked his
mother's face with a long tongue.

5 The Plan

'It's lucky,' said Mr Bear as they drove
towards the Safari Park, 'that it's so near.
We'll be able to visit him regularly.'

'Yes,' said Mrs Bear, reaching back to
pat her son's thick ginger arm, 'and there's
lots of company for him there. The lions,
of course, and they've got tigers too,
and rhinos and elephants and gorillas.'

'*And* bears,' said her husband.

'Yes,' she said. 'I do hope there'll be
some of his own age.'

Mr Bear glanced in the rear-view mirror.
They had stopped on the way for
Mrs Bear to buy Edward a last treat,
a whole honeycomb, and now, Mr Bear
could see, he had finished it, every last
crumb, including the square wooden
frame in which it had been packaged, and
was licking his sticky snout.

'He'll be all right,' he said. 'There'll be
masses of berries and nuts and acorns
and beech-mast and roots, of course,
and grubs and beetles and wasp-nests.

And anyway it'll be winter before long.
Lots of nice snug places to hibernate in
those woods.'

'But he's only got a pair of shorts on.'

Mr Bear looked again at his hairy son.
'Ah,' he said, 'but he's got a good thick
coat.'

How excited Edward was when they
entered the Safari Park — at seeing all the
animals, and at the sight of the woods full
of great trees.

Mr Bear stopped the car near the base

of one of the tallest trees, a monster perhaps thirty metres high. On a branch about halfway up it two bear cubs, just about Edward's age, were sitting, looking down. There was a notice nearby that said:

VISITORS ARE REQUESTED NOT TO LEAVE THEIR CARS UNDER ANY CIRCUMSTANCES. IF IN TROUBLE, SOUND YOUR HORN AND WAIT FOR THE RANGER.

Mr Bear had no intention of sounding his horn. On the contrary, he looked all round very carefully to see that no other cars were in sight.

When he was sure the coast was clear, he leaned back and opened the rear door.

'Out you get, old chap,' he said.

'We'll come and visit you every Saturday, Teddy,' said Mrs Bear.

'And you'll soon be hibernating,' said Mr Bear.

'Have a lovely time,' they said.

Edward gave them each a lick and then
he got out of the car and lolloped happily
off to the bottom of the big tree and began
to climb, whining softly to himself with
pleasure as he saw the two cubs above.

When he had climbed a little way,
he stopped and looked down at the faces
of his parents staring up at him out of the
car windows.

'Cheerio, Edward!' shouted his father.
'See you soon!'

'Goodbye,' called his mother. 'Goodbye,
Teddy.'

And then, with a cheery wave of one
large ginger paw, Teddy Bear turned and
climbed up to meet his newfound friends.